The Magic Pyjamas

by Karen Wallace and
Manola Ca

W

FRANKLIN WATTS

Franklin Watts

First published in Great Britain in 2016 by
The Watts Publishing Group

Series Editor: Jackie Hamley
Series Advisor: Catherine Glavina
Series Designer: Peter Scoulding

A CIP catalogue record for this book is available
from the British Library.

ISBN 978 1 4451 4596 9 hbk)
ISBN 978 1 4451 4589 1 (pbk)
ISBN 978 1 4451 4590 7 (library ebook)

Printed in China

FSC
www.fsc.org
MIX
Paper from
responsible sources
FSC® C104740

Franklin Watts
An imprint of
Hachette Children's Group
Part of The Watts

Alys

Jack was a boy who could
not go to sleep.

He tried counting sheep but that was too difficult.

12

He tried writing, "I will go to sleep!" one hundred times.

But he ran out of paper.

Mum gave him a parrot that said: "Go to sleep! Go to sleep!"

But it flew out the window.

"Why can't you sleep?" asked Dad.

"Sleeping is boring," said Jack. "Nothing ever happens."

No one in the family knew what to do.

13

One day, a parcel arrived.
The note said: "Dear Jack,
These are magic pyjamas.
Love, Granny."

Jack put on the pyjamas and got into bed.

"Nothing magic here," he said. He lay down.

Jack roared off in a plane and landed on a mountain by the sea.

VROOM!

He ran down to the shore and built himself a tree house.

21

Hundreds of birds flew by
and he counted each one.

22

Jack's head was full of amazing pictures.

He yawned and closed his eyes.

"There's no such thing as magic pyjamas," said Dad. "I know," said Mum.

They looked into Jack's bedroom.

The star on his pyjamas glowed in the dark. Jack was asleep!

Puzzle 1

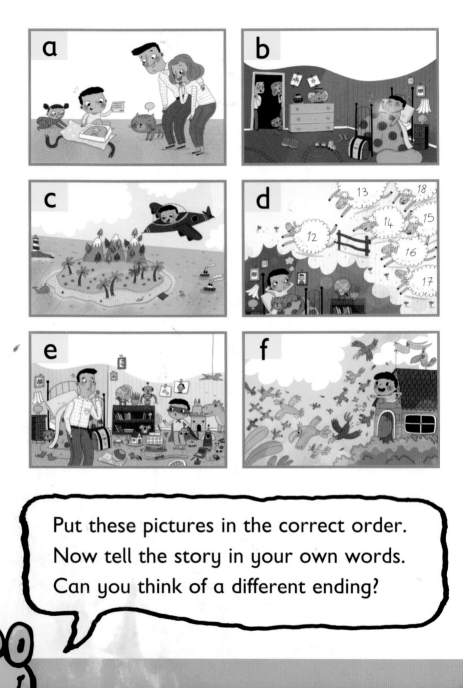

Put these pictures in the correct order.
Now tell the story in your own words.
Can you think of a different ending?

Puzzle 2

bored   cheerful

disinterested

furious   calm

peaceful

Choose the words which best describe
Jack at the beginning and end of the story.
Can you think of any more?

Answers

Puzzle 1

The correct order is:

1d, 2e, 3a, 4c, 5f, 6b

Puzzle 2

Beginning   The correct words are bored, disinterested.
The incorrect word is cheerful.

End   The correct words are calm, peaceful.
The incorrect word is furious.

For details of all our titles go to: www.franklinwatts.co.uk